Dark Man

How many have you read?

Second series

The Dark Candle	978-184167-603-6
The Dark Machine	978-184167-601-2
The Dark Words	978-184167-602-9
Dying for the Dark	978-184167-604-3
Killer in the Dark	978-184167-605-0
The Day is Dark	978-184167-606-7

First series

The Dark Fire of Doom	978-184167-417-9
Destiny in the Dark	978-184167-422-3
The Dark Never Hides	978-184167-419-3
The Face in the Dark Mirror	978-184167-411-7
Fear in the Dark	978-184167-412-4
Escape from the Dark	978-184167-416-2
Danger in the Dark	978-184167-415-5
The Dark Dreams of Hell	978-184167-418-6
The Dark Side of Magic	978-184167-414-8
The Dark Glass	978-184167-421-6
The Dark Waters of Time	978-184167-413-1
The Shadow in the Dark	978-184167-420-9

Dark Man

Killer in the Dark
by Peter Lancett
illustrated by Jan Pedroietta

Published by Ransom Publishing Ltd.
51 Southgate Street, Winchester, Hants. SO23 9EH
www.ransom.co.uk

ISBN   978 184167 605 0

First published in 2007

Copyright © 2007 Ransom Publishing Ltd.

Text copyright © 2007 Peter Lancett
Illustrations copyright © 2007 Jan Pedroietta

Dark Man

Killer in
the Dark

by Peter Lancett

illustrated by Jan Pedroietta

Rans❖m

Chapter One:
Shadow in the Shadows

In the city, the streets are empty.

A cold wind blows. The street lights are all broken.

The Dark Man stands hidden in a doorway, watching.

Across the street is a tower block. It contains flats where the poor and elderly live.

The Dark Man is here because the Old Man asked him to watch over these people.

A foul murderer is on the prowl. Nothing is done to help in this part of the city.

This is why, in the cold and the gloom, the Dark Man watches.

Nothing moves on the street.

The Dark Man's thoughts begin to drift.

He thinks of the girl he still loves. The Shadow Masters took her, a long time in the past.

The thought makes him sad, but brings no tears. He stopped crying long ago.

A car approaches.

The Dark Man shrinks back into the doorway.

The car passes. It is a police car, moving quickly.

The Dark Man knows it will never stop here. No one cares about the people living here.

Across the street there is movement.

A plastic bag flutters from behind an abandoned car.

The Dark Man smiles to himself.

Then he looks again. Something moves behind the car. He cannot tell what it is. It is something black.

A shadow within a shadow.

The shadow moves.

It seems to peel away from the general gloom.
There is no light to cast this shadow.

It seems to be alive.

A chill runs down the Dark Man's spine.

He watches this living darkness as it slides, flat against the wall.

It is shaped like a man, and glides silently towards the tower block entrance. It comes to rest on the glass doors.

The moon appears from behind some clouds. It casts silver light on the shadow.

The shadow leaps as though hurt, then quickly slides down the glass. It slips beneath the doors and into the dark hallway beyond.

The Dark Man can no longer see it.

Chapter Two:
The Girl

The Dark Man hurries across the road.

The glass doors are locked, but he is skilled in the night-time arts. He picks the lock.

Inside the hallway, the gloom casts deep shadows.

It is pitch black beneath the stairwell. The shadow could blend in anywhere.

The Dark Man looks up the stairs. He knows th the shadow will already be creeping up to th flats above.

The Dark Man runs up to the first floor.

Dirty windows let in moonlight. He looks at the patches of black shadow, but sees no movement.

A door opens and a voice whispers, "Quick, over here!"

The voice belongs to a girl.

Outside, clouds hide the moon and the Dark Man can see nothing.

At that moment, the clouds part again. A shaft of moonlight spills onto the landing.

There is movement as something black slides back into the gloom of the stairwell.

The Dark Man is stunned for a moment. He has seen a face melt away with that blackness.

It is the face of the girl he loves.

"Over here!"

It is the girl's voice again. This time it is more urgent.

The Dark Man can just make out an open doorway.

A young woman stands inside.

"Come on, get in here before the moonlight goes."

The Dark Man steps into the flat.

She closes the door behind him.

"Did you see it out there?" the girl asks.

"The living shadow, on the landing before the moonlight came.

"It is afraid of light."

Two candles are burning on a table. They give off just enough light for the Dark Man to see the girl.

She does not face him, but he notices that she seems pretty.

Then she turns towards him.

She has no eyes, just empty black sockets.

Chapter Three:
Here for You

The girl smiles. "Do not feel sorry for me," she says.

The Dark Man looks puzzled.

"I can see it on your face," the girl continues. "The look of pity."

The Dark Man shakes his head. "I don't understand," he says.

The girl smiles.

"I am blind, yes. But I can see in the darkness. I see things in the dark more clearly than you see in the light."

The Dark Man shrugs.

"If this shadow is afraid of light, why don't you switch the lights on?"

"The power comes and goes here. No one cares about fixing it in this part of the city."

The Dark Man looks at the candles.

"Will those protect you?" he asks.

The girl laughs.

"Goodness no. They are not strong enough.
They are here for you."

"But how did you know I was coming?" the
Dark Man asks.

"I can see in the dark. I saw you in the doorway across the road. I saw you follow the shadow."

The shadow!

The Dark Man turns to the door and can just see something black spilling under the gap at the bottom.

He turns to the girl.

"Quick, get near the candles. Make as much light as you can!"

Chapter Four:
A Trick of the Light?

The girl is just standing and grinning at him.

The shadow has slipped past the Dark Man and is attached to her bare feet. It seems like a normal shadow that would be cast by the candles.

Suddenly, the Dark Man understands.

"It is you!" he says. "You are the shadow!"

"It lives my life for me," the girl says.

"I am stuck here, blind. I can go nowhere, experience nothing. Who is there to care for me? At night, the shadow does my living for me."

"But why murder?"

"The shadow needs to feed. It takes worthless souls. Who cares?"

"I care," the Dark Man replies.

Suddenly, the shadow seems to peel away from the girl. It is flat and hangs in the air.

It moves towards the Dark Man.

The Dark Man thrusts his hand inside his pocket. He carries a torch there. The shadow is almost upon him.

He finds the torch, flicks the switch and points it at the shadow.

The light is bright and there is a scream.

The shadow shatters into nothing and the girl slumps to the floor.

For a moment, in the gloom, the Dark Man sees the face of the girl he loves.

But it might be a trick of the light, because quickly, it is just the girl.

She is dead. Her life was linked to the life of the shadow.

The Dark Man leaves the building.

He wonders if the girl was an agent of the Shadow Masters.

Tomorrow, he will ask the Old Man.

The author

photograph: Rachel Ottewill

Peter Lancett is a writer, fiction editor and film maker, living and working in New Zealand and sometimes Los Angeles. He claims that one day he'll 'settle down and get a proper job'.